The Talented
Clementine

The Talented Clementine

SARA PENNYPACKER

PICTURES BY

Marla Frazee

HYPERION BOOKS FOR CHILDREN

New York

For information address Hyperion Books
for Children, 114 Fifth Avenue, New York,
New York 10011-5690.

First edition
3 5 7 9 10 8 6 4 2
This book is set in 15-point Fournier.
Printed in the United States of America
Library of Congress Cataloging-in-Publication Data on file.
ISBN-13: 978-0-7868-3870-7
ISBN-10: 0-7868-3870-1
Reinforced binding
Visit www.hyperionbooksforchildren.com

CHAPTER

I

I have noticed that teachers get *exciting* confused with *boring* a lot. But when my teacher said, "Class, we have an exciting project to talk about," I listened anyway.

"Our school is going to raise money for the big spring trip," he said. "The first and second grades are going to hold a bake sale. The fifth and sixth grades are going to have a car wash. And the third and fourth grades are going to . . . put on a talent show!"

All the kids in the room made sounds as if they

thought a talent show was exciting news. Except me, because it was N-O-T, *not*.

But okay, fine, it wasn't boring, either.

Just then, Margaret's teacher came to the door to talk to my teacher, which was good because it gave me an extra minute to think.

"Old people love to pat my little brother's head," I said when my teacher walked back into the room. "How about we set up a booth and charge them a quarter to do it, instead of having a talent show?"

But he ignored me, which is called Getting on with the Day when a teacher does it, and Being Inconsiderate when a kid does it.

"Class," he said, "one of the fourth graders has come up with a name for our show! Talent-Palooza, Night of the Stars!"

It had to be that Margaret.

"First, we'll need a cooperative group to make some posters. . . ." my teacher said.

And that's when the worried feeling—as if somebody were scribbling with a big black crayon—started up in my brains.

My teacher kept on going with the cooperative group list. The scribbling got harder and faster and spread down into my stomach. I knew what this meant.

I raised my hand.

"Yes, Clementine? Would you like to be in the cooperative group for refreshments?"

"No, thank you," I said, extra politely. "What I'd like is to go to Mrs. Rice's office."

"Clementine, you don't need to go see the principal," my teacher said. "You're not in any trouble."

"Well, it's just a matter of time," I told him.

My teacher looked at me as if he suddenly had

no idea how I'd gotten into his classroom. But then he gave a big sigh and said, "All right," so I got up.

As I left, the O'Malley twins gave me the thumbs-up sign, which made me feel like I wasn't alone. But they were wearing their "Thank goodness it's not me" faces, which made me know that I was.

I walked down the hall on worried legs and knocked on the door with worried knuckles.

"Come in," Principal Rice said. When she saw it was me, she held out her hand for the note from my teacher that would tell her what kind of a little chat we should have. We have done this a lot.

But today I just sat on the chair and started right in. "Which are smarter? Chimpanzees or orangutans?"

"That's an interesting question, Clementine," Mrs. Rice said. "Maybe you could ask the science teacher after you've told me what you're doing here."

"Also, I've been wondering what the difference is between *smashed* and *crashed*."

Mrs. Rice handed me her dictionary.

And then suddenly I didn't want to know anymore! That is the miracle about dictionaries!

"Well, how about you put it on the floor so you can rest your feet on it instead of kicking my desk?" Principal Rice suggested. "You seem to have very busy feet today."

So I did, and it felt good. "Thank you," I said.

"I don't have any talents."

"Excuse me?" said Principal Rice.

"I don't have any talents," I said again.

Mrs. Rice looked at me for a long time and then she said, "Oh."

Then I told her I was all done being there and I left.

When I got off the bus, Margaret's brother, Mitchell, was sitting on the front steps of our apartment building.

"What's the matter, Clementine?" he asked me right away—I guess my worried face was still on.

I handed him the stupid flyer my teacher had sent home with us.

"'Talent-Palooza, Night of the Stars! Share your talents Saturday night!'" he read. Then he handed the stupid flyer back to me. "So, what's the problem?"

I leaned over—but not too close in case he thought I was trying to be his girlfriend, which I am not—and whispered the problem to him.

"I can't hear you," he said.

So I whispered it again.

"I still can't hear you," he said.

So I yelled it.

"That's impossible," he said. "Everybody has a talent."

"Not me."

"No singing?"

"No singing."

"No dancing?"

"No dancing."

"No musical instruments?"

"No musical instruments."

Mitchell was quiet for a minute.

"How about hopping?" he asked finally.

"No hopping," I answered.

"Everyone can hop," Mitchell said.

"Not me." Then I proved it to him.

"Wow," said Mitchell. Twice.

I sat down on the step beside him. Except I fell

off, because my body was a little confused from trying to hop. "See?" I said. "I can't even do sitting. It's hopeless."

"Maybe not. Cheer up. Maybe you have a really great talent you just haven't figured out yet."

I gave Mitchell a "See? I'm cheered up already!" smile. But it was just my mouth pretending.

The next morning, Margaret sat next to me on the bus as usual. I had never noticed it before, but she was very talented at sitting down: her dress stayed in place as if it were painted on, and not a single paper spilled out of her backpack.

Which reminded me to crawl under the seat to get all mine before we got to the school. This is called Being Organized.

The O'Malley twins got on at the next stop and sat in front of us. They are named Willy and Lilly. When I first heard about this idea, I tried to get my parents to change my brother's name so it would rhyme with mine. "How about Blementine?" I asked them. "How about Frementine, or Shlementine?"

But they weren't interested, so I just keep calling him vegetable names, which are the only ones worse than a fruit name, like I got stuck with.

Lilly turned around. "What are you going to do at the talent show, Margaret?" she asked.

"I have too many talents!" Margaret groaned. She flapped her hands around her head as if her talents were flies she had to shoo away. "Hundreds of them! I can't decide!"

This was true. Margaret was always taking lessons: clarinet, baton twirling, ballet, swimming . . . you name it, she took lessons for it.

"Why don't you do them all at once?" I suggested. Which was supposed to be a joke. And okay, fine, not the nice kind.

But Margaret was not very talented at knowing when I was joking.

"That's a wonderful idea, Clementine! Thank you!"

Then the O'Malley twins and I had to listen for a hundred hours to Margaret figuring out which talents would be good together. Ice skating and accordion-playing probably wouldn't work. But tap dancing and singing would be easy, and she could Hula-Hoop at the same time. Plus, she could play a drum if she hung it around her neck. And maybe throw in a couple of cartwheels.

"And hey!" she cried, slapping her forehead at the great idea that had just popped in. "What if I rode a *horse* onstage?!"

"Well, I've only got one talent," Willy said. "But it's a great one!" He lifted his lunch box. "My whole lunch. In my mouth. At once."

"You do that every day," I reminded him.

"Not onstage," Willy answered.

Then he asked me what I was going to do.

"It's a surprise," my mouth said without me even telling it to. Which was not a lie, because if I did anything at all up on that stage next weekend, it would be a pretty big surprise, all right.

And then I pressed my mouth into a ruler line for the rest of the bus ride so it couldn't say any more surprises.

In school, my teacher started in with the "Talent-Palooza" business so fast I thought it was the new last part of the Pledge of Allegiance.

"With liberty and justice for all and I know we're all very excited to get to our big project," he said. So it was too late for my secret plan of hypnotizing him into forgetting.

Luckily, I thought up another really good plan right away. I raised my hand.

16

"Yes, Clementine? Do you want to volunteer for a cooperative group?"

"I would like to tell something to you," I answered. I made a capital *P* with my fingers which means "in *private*."

My teacher nodded, so I went up to his desk. I made quick secret-eyes all around behind there to look for the pizza and doughnuts everyone knows teachers eat when kids aren't looking, but I didn't find any. Then I told him what I was thinking up.

"What if there's a kid who doesn't have any talent? Not me, because I have L-O-T-S, *lots*. Of course. I have *so* many. But what if some *other* kid doesn't?"

"Everyone has a talent, Clementine," my teacher

answered. "Everyone has something they're especially good at."

"But what if one kid got left out? What if whoever's in charge forgot to give one kid a talent? Wouldn't that person who is not me be embarrassed at a talent show?"

"Why, that's very thoughtful of you," my teacher said. "But . . ."

"Yep," I said, "I am very thoughtful. So I guess we should just forget about that whole Talent-Palooza idea."

"Oh, I really don't think so. But just to be sure, I'll talk to the class." Then he stood and said, "Class, let's have a show of hands. How many of you have an act to perform at the talent show?"

Everyone's hand shot up in the air.

"Well, I guess that settles that," my teacher said. "But thank you anyway, Clementine."

Okay, fine, it wasn't such a good idea.

But just then, an even better one popped into my head. I'm lucky that way: astoundishing ideas are always popping into my head, and I don't even have to use my brains to get them there.

At journal writing I did my idea. When I was done writing, I curled my hand over my sentence, as if it were too private to share. Which is how you get a teacher to come and look at it.

Sure enough, my teacher came over and took a look. He frowned and bent closer to read it again.

"You have to move this week?"

I quick squeezed the word *might* in between *I* and *have to move this week. Might* is a helpful word when you are not exactly telling the truth.

"You *might* have to move?"

I nodded. Nodding is not exactly telling a lie.

"Where might you have to move to?"

I had forgotten to think about this part.

"Ummmm . . ." While I was umming I looked around the room in case there was a good answer lying around. And there was! I pointed to the social studies bulletin board we had made last week.

"You're moving to *Egypt?*" my teacher asked.

I nodded again. You never know.

"Why?" my teacher asked. "Is one of your parents being transferred?"

I was glad he had thought of this good reason. "My dad," I said. "He might be getting a new job."

My dad is a building manager. He makes sure

everything runs okay in our building, which has lots of apartments. Last year our building went condo. This means that now the apartments are called condominiums and the people own them instead of renting them. My dad says sometimes they get a little confused and think it means they own *him*. He's not so crazy about buildings going condo.

"He might have to take care of a pyramid!" I said.

I pointed to the cardboard pyramid Willy O'Malley had made. If I had made it, it would have had the right number of sides. But I was stuck drawing the Sphinx because whenever anyone else tried it looked like a grasshopper.

When I draw things, everyone knows what they are. Even grown-ups. This is because I am practically a famous artist. If they had a game show for drawing I would probably win every prize. And I

would not pick the dumb ones like dining-room
sets or a year's supply of car wax, either.

"Don't you think it's unfair that game shows
don't have good prizes, like gorillas or sub-
marines?" I asked my teacher.

But he wasn't paying attention. "Your father
is being transferred to a pyramid? Is he an
archaeologist, Clementine?"

"He's a building manager. He says everything's going condo these days. He says nothing's safe. The Great Pyramid is four hundred eighty-one-feet tall. That's as tall as a fifty-story building. That could be a lot of condominiums."

"And your father's going to go over there and manage them?"

"*Might*," I reminded him. "It's a big job. He'd have to do things like hire the doormen, and make sure the elevators run right. So I guess I won't be here for the . . ."

"Elevators? In the Great Pyramid?"

"Yep. And tell people, 'No grills on the roof!' That's another part of his job. Anyway, it's too bad that I can't be in the Talent-Pa—"

"No grills on the roof of the Great Pyramid?"

"Right. And, 'Please leave your trash outside on Thursdays!' So I'm really sad that . . ."

But my teacher just patted my head. "You are

one in a million, Clementine, one in a million."
Then he was all done being at my desk and he
walked away, laughing.

There should be a rule about that. No laughing
for teachers.

3

When I got off the bus, I saw my dad outside, trimming the ivy that grows between our building and the sidewalk.

He pointed to an extra pair of clippers beside him. "You're eight now, Sport. I think you're old enough to handle these."

So I picked up the clippers, even though I am not so fond of pointy things, and started trimming the ivy with him.

After a couple of minutes, he said, "You were

kind of quiet at dinner last night. Is anything wrong?"

I wanted to tell him about having no talents for the talent show. But just then the junior high bus pulled up and Mitchell got off. He came over and asked what we were doing.

"Got to keep after this ivy," my dad told him. "It grows so fast it could cover the windows and be all over the sidewalk if I don't keep cutting it back."

Mitchell dropped his backpack. "Whoa," he said. "Do you mean that if one of the Red Sox was walking by, and the ivy was shooting out onto the sidewalk, it could trip him? And then he'd be out for the rest of the season? And then we might not be in the play-offs, or the World Series?"

"Well, that's not exactly the reason the condo association gave," my dad said. "But I like your reason better: we're playing an important role in the outcome of baseball history this year." He held his clippers out. "Want to help?"

"Whoa," Mitchell said again. "Dude." He high-fived my dad, then took the clippers. "Thanks!"

Mitchell began trimming the ivy, and my dad sat down on the brick wall to rest. They started talking about baseball.

We live in Boston, and Mitchell is obsessed with the Red Sox. He's going to be one when he's older. If I ever get married, which I will not, I would like to marry a Red Sox player, but not Mitchell, because he's not my boyfriend. Then you could get all those hot dogs for free in the ball park.

"Did you ever see a strike-out perfect game?" my dad was asking Mitchell. "I did once, in the minor leagues. It's a thing of beauty."

"What's a strike-out perfect game?" I asked.

"It's when a pitcher throws only strikes for a whole game," Mitchell told me.

"Wow," I said. "So, eighty-one strikes in a row!" Mitchell stared at me, and you could tell he was trying to multiply strikes and outs and innings in his head.

"Don't bother," my dad told him. "She's a genius at math."

"Whoa," Mitchell said for the third time. "Awesome." Then he walked off, shaking his head, probably to try it on a calculator.

Dad picked up the clippers and got back to work. "So," he asked again. "Is everything all right, Sport?"

"Well, I was wondering if we might be moving."

"Moving?" he repeated.

"Right," I said. "I was just wondering if you might be getting a new job. In Egypt."

"You thought I might be getting a new job in Egypt?"

I nodded. "On Friday."

"Well, that's an odd one. No. You don't have to worry about that anymore. We are definitely not moving to Egypt on Friday. In fact, we have no plans to move anywhere, any time."

Then we trimmed the ivy some more. And I got a good idea.

My dad says I'm the queen of noticing interesting things. He says he's just learning from a master, but I think he's pretty good at it too. For a grown-up, anyway.

So I asked him if he'd noticed any good talents lately.

"What do you mean?"

"Well, not the normal ones, like singing or dancing or playing an instrument. Those are boring. I was just wondering if you've seen any pizazzy ones lately."

"Well, let's see. In the park this morning, I saw a bunch of guys flying kites with fishing poles. They were really good—really talented at it."

That would be kind of hard on a stage. "Any other ones?"

"Well, on the way home, I was walking behind a woman. She had a poodle, a pocketbook, and a cup of coffee and she was talking on her phone. I have no idea how she juggled all that."

Juggling was a good talent.

"Thanks, Dad!" I said.

Then I went inside. Luckily, I found everything right away. My mom's pocketbook was right on her drawing table, and next to it was half a cup of coffee. The phone was under my bed—probably String Bean left it there, because I'm sure I didn't. Then I found Moisturizer and scooped him up.

Okay, fine, a kitten isn't the same as a poodle. This is called Making Do.

Let me tell you, it's pretty hard just holding all those things at once. And before I could toss everything into the air and start talking on the phone, Moisturizer saw a bird outside the window. He jumped out of my arms, and everything else crashed to the floor.

And I learned the difference between *crashed* and *smashed*: crashed is easier to clean up. Also, I

learned that coffee is easier to clean up when you spill it on a new brown rug. You hardly have to touch it at all!

I went back outside and asked my dad if he had any other talents to tell me about.

He put down his clippers. "Why all this interest in talent all of a sudden, Sport?"

I reached into my pocket and pulled out the stupid flyer and handed it to him.

"'Talent-Palooza, Night of the Stars,'" he read. "That's quite a title."

I pointed up to the fifth floor.

"Oh," he said. "Margaret."

I nodded. "And Margaret has hundreds of talents. She's going to do something really pizazzy at the show."

"So you're trying to think up something pizazzy to do, too, right?"

"Not exactly," I said. "I'm trying to think up anything to do at all. I don't have any talents."

"Are you kidding, Clementine? You're the most talented person I know!"

Of course, he has to say that: he's my father. Still, for a minute I started thinking maybe he and Mitchell were right. Maybe I had some really great talent I just didn't know about yet. Then he started talking again and ruined it.

"Take pruning ivy, for instance," he said, nodding at my wall. "You're a natural. One day, and you're already one of the best in the business, Sport."

"Dad." My dad thinks he's funny. Mostly I do, too.

"Or thinking of things to put on top of toast. Remember the lime Jell-O? I still can't get over it. Sheer genius."

"Dad. I'm serious."

"Okay, seriously. Let's see. You're good at math, obviously. You're an amazing artist. And you're really good at seeing things from a fresh angle, having new ideas. Remember how you won the Great Pigeon War for me? And you're the queen of noticing things. You're curious and you ask the most interesting questions. You—"

"Dad!" I stopped him. "I can't do those things on a stage!"

But he wasn't paying attention. "And you are very empathetic. Do you know what that means?"

I shook my head. Maybe it was something like "good at a musical instrument nobody knows about."

My dad sat down on the wall again and patted a space next to him. I sat down, too.

"It's a wonderful thing to be. It means you're

good at figuring out how other people are feeling.
You care about that."

And suddenly I was very empathetic! I saw that
my dad was starting to get worried about me. And
he was going to feel sad if he couldn't help me.

So I jumped up. "Thanks, Dad! I feel better now!" I gave him a big smile and hurried inside in case he was empathetic, too. In case he could see what I was really feeling.

CHAPTER

4

Wednesday morning, Margaret's teacher came
into our classroom right after the pledge, to visit
with my teacher. This is because the fourth graders
are supposed to be responsible enough to be left
alone for a few minutes. I don't think this is such a
hot idea. I know Margaret and I never leave her
alone in my room.

But I was glad. Margaret's teacher wears her
hair swirled up like a tornado, and I think if a
bobby pin ever came shooting out of it, it would
look like lightning. I like watching for that.

"I am going to be the director of our talent show," Margaret's teacher said. "Each morning we'll have a little trial run of a couple of acts. That way everything will run smoothly on the big night."

My teacher made a face at Margaret's teacher. It meant they didn't believe that for a minute, but they had to say it anyway.

"Who would like to go first today?"

All the kids except me raised their hands, so my teacher just started with the first row.

"My act is called 'Cartwheel Extravaganza,'" said Maria.

She went up to the front of the classroom and did a cartwheel into the chalkboard. We were all very surprised to learn that a chalkboard that big wouldn't flatten a kid when it fell off the wall.

"Are you all right?" my teacher asked, lifting it off her.

"Oh, sure," said Maria. "I always do that."

"Well, just in case, why don't you go visit the nurse. And we'll make sure there are no chalk-boards on the stage Saturday night." Then he called on the next kid, whose name is Morris or Boris, I always forget.

"My act is named 'Cartwheel Wham-o-Rama,'" Morris-Boris said. He jumped up out of his seat.

"Wait, no!" my teacher cried, throwing his arms around the fish tank.

But it was too late. Morris-Boris cartwheeled to the front of the room, where he didn't knock over the fish tank, thank goodness, only the hamster cage. Zippy and Bump looked pretty surprised to be out on the floor like that and they let Morris-Boris scoop them right up.

"Thank you, Norris," my teacher said. "Are you all right?"

Oh. I wrote a big *N* on my arm so I wouldn't forget.

"We'll make sure there are no hamster cages on the stage, either. And just to be on the safe side, why don't you go visit the nurse, too."

I don't know why my teacher bothered with sending Maria and Norris to the nurse. All she ever does when you go in to tell her how sick you are is roll her eyes. She always looks bored, as if she's just killing time until a really good disease hits the school. Maria and Norris could have head lumps the size of toasters, and all our nurse would do is hand them a frozen sponge.

"Now," my teacher was saying, "does anyone have an act that *isn't* cartwheeling?"

Half the kids put their hands down. My teacher

called on a boy named Joe and asked him what his act was.

Secretly I was hoping it was cartwheeling anyway. Joe is really short and he has really short everything: really short name, really short hair, really short ears. He has really short arms and legs, too, so if he did a cartwheel, I bet it would look like a starfish rolling across the floor, and I would like to see that.

But nope.

Joe took a harmonica from his pocket. "I'm going to play this. And my dog, Buddy, is going to sing."

"Your dog?" my teacher asked. "Your dog sings?"

Joe went over to the open window and whistled. His big brown dog, who waits all day on the playground for him, ran over. He jumped up and put his paws on the window ledge. Then Joe blew into his harmonica.

Buddy threw back his big brown dog head, closed his eyes, and howled.

"See?" said Joe. "Buddy loves my harmonica-playing!"

"Well, I don't know . . ." my teacher started.

Then Margaret's teacher came over and wrote something in her notebook and showed it to my teacher. I guess it was, "At least it's not cartwheels!" because then my teacher said, "Okay. Two rules. First, Buddy has to be on a leash. And second, if he has an accident on the stage, you have to clean it up."

Joe said okay, and then my teacher said, "That's enough for one day, time for social studies," which was lucky because I was the next person in the row.

But I couldn't stop thinking about not having an act to do. My teacher had to say six "Clementine-you-need-to-pay-attention!"s, which is a lot, even for me.

By the time the bus came, I was so tired from worrying that my neck felt too weak to hold up my head. I flopped over in the seat.

"What's the matter?" Margaret asked me. "Are you sick?"

"I might be," I said.

"Well, I hope you're not too sick to come to the talent show Saturday night. You'd miss my act. Which would be a shame, because you could really use it."

I perked up a little. "What do you mean? What's your act?"

"The name of it is 'Dressing Fashionably,'" Margaret said.

"That's not an act!"

"It is too. And it's something I'm very talented at. And certain people are not." Margaret pointed her eyes at me at the "certain people" part.

"What about all your other talents? What about gymnastics and singing and playing the accordion?"

"Oh, lots of kids can do those things. Dressing Fashionably is a very special talent. And besides, my act will be helpful to certain people." She arrow-eyed me at the "certain people" part again, but I didn't care. Because I thought of something.

"Can I have one of your extra talents, then?" I asked her. "One of the ones you're not going to do?"

Margaret squinted at me.

"Can you show me how to do one? As long as you're not going to be performing it . . ."

Margaret thought for a minute. Then she said, "Well, okay. I guess we can *try*. Come over tomorrow after school."

5

Finally, Thursday after-school came.

"We'll go through my talents alphabetically," said Margaret.

She went to a shelf and pulled down her accordion. She looked at my hands and then she looked at the keys. She put the accordion back. "Fingerprints," she said.

Then she handed me her baton. Which I dropped.

"Baton twirling's out."

"How about your clarinet?" I asked.

Margaret shook her head. "Spit."

"*D* is for dramatic acting class," she told me. "Pretend you've just heard some surprising news."

I clapped my hands to the sides of my face and made my mouth a capital *O*.

"Dramatic acting's out, too," Margaret decided.

E was for riding English, and Margaret said I needed a horse for that. *F* was for fencing, and she said I wasn't mature enough to touch her sword. I was losing hope, but then finally, when she got to *T*, she brightened up.

"Tap dancing!"

"Tap dancing's easy?" I asked.

"Oh, no," she said. "Tap dancing is really hard. But maybe you could fake it. Maybe you could just kind of clomp around in tap shoes making a lot of noise."

"I can clomp around," I agreed. "So I just need some tap shoes!"

"You can wear my old ones," Margaret said.

Then she took me into her closet, which looks like a clothing store: everything is all folded perfectly and hung up in neat lines. In Margaret's closet you expect to see signs saying BIG SALE ON SWEATERS! or NEW FASHION ARRIVALS! There was a whole wall of cubbies just for shoes, and every pair was in its own plastic bag.

I pointed to the bags. "How come?"

"Germs!" Margaret shuddered and made a face like she'd just swallowed a toad.

"In or out?" I asked.

"In or out, what?"

"The germs. Are you keeping them in or out?"

Margaret glared at me as if this question was too dumb to bother with, but I don't think she knew the answer.

She picked out a bag and started to give it to me,

then stopped. "Have you washed your hands? You have to wash your hands." She pointed to the bathroom.

I went into her bathroom, which is hers alone and she doesn't even have to share it with a brother, like I do.

Margaret's bathroom looks like a bathroom store. Okay, fine, I've never seen a bathroom store, but it would probably look just like this, except it would have price tags on the faucet and the soap and the toilet paper.

I looked at my hands. They looked really good to me. Plus, they felt just right—not too slippery, not too sticky. And best of all they smelled perfect: a mixture of my new drawing pencils and grape bubble gum. It's hard to get your hands to smell perfect like that.

So I only pretended to wash them. I have invented a good way to do this.

First, you run the water. Then you hold the soap under the faucet so it gets wet, then put it back. Then you get the towel, and here is the tricky part: you can't get it too wet but you can't leave it dry, either. So what I invented is this: dab the towel into the wet sink just a little bit, then hang it back up. But rumpled, this time.

I did all this, then I walked back into Margaret's room and took off my shoes.

Margaret's eyes grew so big I thought they were going to sproing out on stalks, like cartoon eyes.

"Clementine!" she gasped. "Your feet are huge!"

"Shhhhh!" I hushed her, in case Mitchell was hanging around listening to us.

Margaret put her foot next to mine. "Well, they're as big as mine now. These aren't going to fit," she warned me.

I tried to fit my feet into Margaret's old tap shoes anyway, but it was no use. I felt very empathetic about Cinderella's stepsisters.

I was so sad I flopped down on Margaret's bed before I remembered the rule about that.

"Wrinkles!" Margaret screamed. She ran over and pushed me off the bed, then smoothed the bedspread, which has poodles wearing hats on it.

So I sat on her chair to be sad there, instead.

I studied the bottoms of Margaret's tap shoes. "If I nailed something tappy into the bottoms of my sneakers, that would work, wouldn't it? I just need to make the sound, don't I?"

"Well," said Margaret. "I guess."

"I'll be right back."

Then I took the elevator all the way down to *B* for basement, because I knew exactly what would make that tappy sound.

Once a month, all the

people who own condominiums in our building get together to argue about what things they need to buy for the building and who should pay how much. They drink beer at these meetings. My dad says this is not such a hot idea because then they forget what they decided, but he's only the manager of the building, so he can't tell them what to do. He just lets them keep the beer in the basement.

And all those beers came in bottles. With bottle caps.

I got a pair of pliers from the workbench. Let me tell you, it is N-O-T, *not* easy to get twenty-four bottle caps off with a pair of pliers, but finally I did it. Luckily, most of the beer that spilled soaked into my clothes, so I only had to mop up a small puddle.

Then I went back to the workbench. I got out my dad's building manager–strength superglue

and glued all the bottle caps to the soles of my sneakers. All the while, I kept smiling whenever I thought about how happy everyone would be next week at the meeting because their bottles had already been opened!

When I was done, I put my sneakers on and a good surprise happened. It was hard to walk, but when I did, I sounded exactly like a person tap dancing! I pushed the elevator button for the fifth floor so I could show Margaret.

The elevator stopped at the lobby floor and Margaret's mother and Alan got in.

Alan is Margaret's mother's boyfriend. Margaret and Mitchell are not so happy about this because Alan kisses Margaret's mother in public. Margaret and Mitchell think there should be a rule about grown-ups kissing in public if any of them are your parents. This is the only thing they have ever agreed about in their entire lives.

"Hi there, Tangerine!" Alan said.

Alan thinks he is funny. I do not.

Alan sniffed the air as if he were smelling something weird. Then he bent over and sniffed me. "What the . . . ?"

Margaret's mother bent over and sniffed me, too. "*Beer?*" she said. She reached out and stabbed the STOP ELEVATOR button, then she punched the button for my floor. "I think we need to pay a little visit to your parents, Clementine."

6

My mother opened the door, and Margaret's mother handed me over.

"Oh, thank you so much, Susan!" my mother said, as if it was a wonderful surprise. Then she closed the door.

While I was explaining, she did so many "Clementine-what-were-you-thinking?"s that I finally stopped counting them.

Then my dad came in and she told him about it, except she couldn't finish her sentences.

"All twenty-four . . . Condo Association meeting

. . . Glued them on . . . Spilled all over . . . Smells like beer . . . !!!"

Somehow my dad understood, and then I had to listen to all *his* "Clementine-what-were-you-thinking?"s, too.

"And besides all that," my mother said when he was done, "her sneakers are ruined."

"Let me have them," my dad said. "Maybe I can get those bottle caps off."

"No, Dad!" I cried. "I need them for my act! I'm tap-dancing at the talent show!"

Too late. My dad left. But I was in luck—a few minutes later he came back, holding my sneakers. With the bottle caps still on.

"They wouldn't come off?" my mother asked.

"Not in this lifetime," my father answered.

"Are you saying . . . ?" my mother began.

Then they stared at each other and they both said, "Not me!" at the same time.

"I took her last month," said my mom.

"I won't do it this time," I told them. "I'll be like a normal person."

My mother and father just looked at me as if I'd spoken in Martian, which I am going to learn. Then they turned back to each other.

"I really think I should stay here," said my dad. "What if the elevator breaks again and I have to call the repair service?"

"But what if someone needs a drawing really, really fast—an emergency piece of art?" my mother tried. "No, I'd better stay home."

"If you take her, I'll make dinner every night for a week," my father offered.

"I'll make dinner every night for two weeks," said my mother. "And do the dishes."

My parents always try to bribe each other into taking me shopping, which I do not think is funny. But—okay, fine—I take a really, really long time in stores. My parents think I have a hard time choosing things, but that's not it. I can choose things just fine. The problem is, whenever you have to choose something, that means you have to not-choose about a hundred other things. Which is not so easy.

Like in the candy store. If you choose peanut butter cups you have to not-choose red licorice and M&M's and Starbursts and bubble gum. And Tootsie Rolls and Gummi Worms and Pixy Stix.

And no matter what you pick, as soon as you take the first bite, you suddenly know you wanted one of the other ones.

Still, this time I could try. "Today," I promised my parents, "I'll be really quick."

My parents just made faces that said, "We've heard that joke before." Then my mom sent me to my room to change into dry overalls. When I got back, they were still at it.

"I will make dinner and do the dishes for three weeks," said my father.

"A month," said my mother.

I flopped down on the couch to wait. When they got going like this, it could take a while.

Finally, my father took all the money out of his wallet and held it out to my mother. "If you take her, you could buy a pair of shoes, too. My treat."

My mother said, "Well . . ." and I could see she was thinking about it.

And then my father said, "Plus, I'll take you out to dinner so you can wear them."

My mother reached toward the money, then stopped. "We're not talking pizza or hamburgers, right?"

"Absolutely not," promised my dad. "We're talking a tablecloth-and-candles kind of place."

"It might even be . . . the Ritz," my mother warned him.

The Ritz is the fanciest restaurant in Boston. It is very expensive, probably because it costs a lot to make all those crackers.

"A deal," my dad said.

My parents smiled at each other and then they kissed. And here is a secret thing that I never tell Margaret or Mitchell—I like it when my parents kiss. Even in public.

On the way to the shoe store, whenever we slowed down a little bit, people on the sidewalk would sniff at me and wrinkle their noses. "It's not what you think," my mother said every time. Then she made me walk even faster, which is not easy when you have twenty-four bottle caps on the soles of your shoes.

When we got into the store, right away I saw a great pair of bright green sneakers in the front window. I ran in and climbed up to get them.

My mother grabbed me by my overalls and pulled me back. "That's the display window,

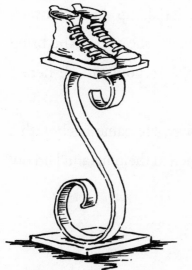

Clementine. We need to find a salesman."

And you will not believe how lucky I was, because right then I found one! He came running up behind me.

"May I show you something?" he asked, with a nervous look on his face.

I pointed to the bright green sneakers and my mother said, "Size three and a half."

"Wonderful," said the salesman. "That's the lime from our new 'Popsicle' line. It also comes in—"

"No!" My mother tried to stop him. "That's fine, please don't tell us the other—"

Too late.

"Lemon, orange, coconut, grape, blueberry, mango, and pink grapefruit. Very popular."

My mother threw her hands up and then sank into a chair. "Bring them all," she said. "And bring them in size four, too. We're going to be here a long time."

The salesman went away. He came back with a big stack of boxes. He opened them up and laid out all the pairs in front of me in a big sneaker rainbow. Then he sniffed. He looked at my mother as if he couldn't believe what his nose just told him.

"It's not what you think." My mother slumped down in her chair and sighed. "Oh, heck," she said. "Maybe it is what you think."

I tried on all the Popsicle sneakers.

The salesman asked me if I really had to test out each color by running across the store, climbing onto a chair, and then jumping off. I guess he was new.

Blueberry was the zoomiest, and pink grapefruit was the bounciest, so I put one on each foot and tried them out together. It was perfect and it looked wonderful, too, but the salesman said, "I don't think so."

And I didn't even care, because right then I saw

the most beautiful pair
of shoes in the world
on a shelf near the
display window: pur-
ple, with tall, skinny
high heels and sparkly green dragonflies at
the toes.

I pointed to them. "How about . . . ?" and
before I could finish, both the salesman and my
mom said, "I don't think so," at the same time.

"Okay, fine," I said. "What other kinds of shoes
do you have in this store?"

"I can't watch this," said my mother. "Just make
sure she chooses something sensible." She got up
and whispered to the salesman. Then she went
over to the grown-up shoes and started shopping.

As soon as she was gone, I asked the salesman if
he had a tattoo. You can never tell which adults are
going to have one.

"No," said the salesman. "Do you?"

"Not yet," I said. "Pretty soon."

Then he left to get some more shoes for me. And you would not believe how many pairs of shoes were in that store! My feet were exhausted from all the trying on and my head hurt from all the not-choosing I was thinking about.

Finally, the salesman held up a pair of striped basketball sneakers. "This is it," he said. "These are the last shoes we've got."

When he was lacing them up for me, I saw something amazing. "Hey, did you know that you have a circle right at the top of your head where there's no hair?" I asked him.

"Yes," he said, "I am aware of that, thank you. Did you know that you smell like a brewery?"

"Yes," I said, "I am aware of that, thank you. And I'll take the lime Popsicle sneakers."

The salesman sighed. "I know that, too," he said. "They're already in the bag at the checkout counter. Your mother told me you'd end up picking them."

Then I went up to the register where my mother was waiting. I made my mouth into a ruler line because I was so mad at her for knowing what I was going to do before I did. I was never going to speak to her again.

"Want to see what I bought?" my mother asked outside.

I kept my mouth a ruler line but I nodded and opened up her bag.

And then I didn't care about being mad. "WOW!" I said.

"Exactly," she said. "Wow."

We stopped and just stared at those purple wow shoes. The heels looked even taller and skinnier, and the dragonflies sparkled in the sun like emeralds. They were so beautiful that I was suddenly cured of being afraid of pointy things.

"Not very sensible," I said.

"No, definitely not very sensible," my mom agreed. "In fact, they're probably the least sensible shoes in the store. One of the benefits of being a grown-up."

"Can I try them on?"

"Sure," she said. Then she leaned over and gave me a huge smiling hug, even though I smelled like a brewery! "*After* you've had a bath."

I showed Margaret my new sneakers at the bus stop Friday morning.

"Oh, yeah," she said. She fake yawned. "I had a pair like that when I was a little kid. Not green, though. Green is the dumbest color."

That Margaret.

When I got on the bus, I hid my feet under my backpack and looked out the window for the whole ride. There are ninety-four street lamps between the bus stop and the school.

In my classroom, a surprise was waiting: we had a substitute. Mrs. Righty-O. I call her that because she always says "Righty-O." Also, okay, fine, because I can't ever remember her name.

It was a good surprise for two reasons. First, because when she read my teacher's instructions, she said, "I'm sorry, but we're not going to be able to have a run-through of the last acts for the talent show. It will be a miracle if I can even figure out what the heck we're supposed to be doing for class work."

The second reason was that seeing Mrs. Righty-O in the front of the room gave me the most astoundishing idea of my entire life.

I raised my hand. "Yes?" Mrs. Righty-O said.

"I need to go to the principal's office," I told her.

"Righty-O," Mrs. Righty-O said. Substitutes don't ask you *why* about things.

I walked down the hall, which was very hard because my new sneakers wanted to run, and I knocked on Mrs. Rice's door.

"I have new sneakers," I told Mrs. Rice.

"I see that," she said. "Do you have a note?"

"Nope. I just came to tell you that tomorrow night I'll be sending in a substitute."

"A substitute?"

"Right. A substitute. Like my teacher sent a substitute today."

"I'm sorry, but there are no substitute students."

"But why not? If a teacher can have a substitute teacher, how come a kid can't have a substitute kid?"

Mrs. Rice looked at me for a long time. "Do you know, Clementine, that no one has ever asked that question before? And it's a good question. An excellent question.

"I'm sorry that the answer is still no, but I'm going to need a little time to come up with an excellent reason for you."

"Oh. So am I all done being here?" I asked.

"You're all done being here," Mrs. Rice answered. "For now."

After school, I brought my old sneakers with the new tappy bottoms up to Margaret's apartment.

"All right. I'll teach you a very easy routine," Margaret said. "But remember, you have to do everything I say. You're eight and I'm nine, so that means I'm the boss of you."

Which is a rule I don't like very much.

"What about Mitchell?" I asked. "He's older than you. Is he the boss of you?"

"Mitchell is Mitchell," Margaret said. "He can't be the boss of anybody."

"Well, what about my parents, then? I guess they're the boss of all of us."

"Nope," Margaret said. "My mom is way older than your parents. She's the boss. So you have to do what I say."

Sometimes that Margaret makes me so mad. I tried one more thing. "Oh, yeah? Well, what about Mrs. Jacobi on the top floor? She's about a hundred, and I think that's older than your mother, so that makes her the boss."

Margaret looked stumped for a minute. "I don't

know," she admitted. "It's too hard to tell with grown-ups." Then she brightened up. "So we'll just stick to me being the boss of you."

I thought about the talent show. And about me being the only one without any talents.

"Okay, fine," I said. "For today."

Margaret put on her tap shoes, and I put on my sneakers with the bottle caps. She rolled up her rug and started tapping around.

"This is called Shuffle off to Buffalo," she said. "I am extremely wonderful at it. Just do what I do."

Except she did four million things at once.

"Head high, spine straight, arms floating, big smile!" Margaret said. "Flap, flap, step, step, ball-shuffle, change!"

Her feet were moving so fast I couldn't even see them, but I went over to the floor to try it anyway.

Let me tell you, a shiny wooden floor is very slippery when you have twenty-four bottle caps glued to your sneakers. I took one step onto it and skidded right into Margaret's dressing table. Perfume bottles and hair clips and brushes and rings and ribbons went flying through the air.

Margaret made a face that said, "Clementine, you are hopeless."

Which I already knew.

But then while she was picking everything up, she surprised me.

"I guess you're not meant for tap dancing," she said. "But we still have a little time. I'll keep trying to think up something you could be not so hopeless at."

I think Margaret might be a little empathetic, too.

"Thanks for the lesson, anyway," I told her.

I changed back into my new sneakers and went outside to where my dad was finishing up the ivy. Maybe he'd noticed some really great new talent today. But before I could tell him the bad news that his daughter was a failure at tap dancing, my brother came outside with my mom. He ran over to us and tried to pick up my dad's clippers.

"Uh-unh," Dad said. "Sorry, Bud—not for little guys."

Cabbage screwed up his face like we were in for a real wail, so I quickly stuck some ivy into my sleeves and down my neck and waved my arms at him. I went staggering around crying, "Help! Help! I swallowed some ivy seeds!" This made him laugh so hard he forgot all about the wailing.

"Now, that!" my dad cried. "See? There's another talent you have, Clementine! Nobody else in the world can make your brother laugh like that."

"Dad," I reminded him. "That's not something people perform on a stage."

And then I remembered Joe. "Hey, Mom," I said. "Could Beets still have an accident?"

"First of all, your brother's name isn't Beets. And second of all, what do you mean, an accident?"

"I mean, he doesn't ever need diapers anymore,
right? Even if he heard a really loud sound, like,
say, clapping—he'd be okay, he wouldn't . . . ?"

"Oh. No, he's pretty safe there. Clementine, you ask the most interesting questions."

Then she dragged my brother off for his playgroup while he was still laughing about the ivy.

I thought about the other part. My teacher probably wouldn't make me put a leash on my brother. But I wasn't so sure about Margaret's teacher. Margaret's teacher really liked rules. "Do we have a leash?" I asked my dad.

"A leash? No, of course not. Why do you want one?"

"Do you know anybody who does? I just need to borrow one for a little while."

"Well, actually, I've seen a leash in Mrs. Jacobi's storage compartment. From when she had that Dalmatian. You could ask her."

My dad knows everything about everybody in the building, and he's always saying it's a good thing he can keep a secret.

"But Clementine, I don't think Moisturizer would like that."

"Dad! I know that! I would never put a leash on a *cat*!"

CHAPTER
8

At breakfast Saturday, I reminded my parents about the talent show. "You're going to be there, right? It's at six o'clock. You're going to be there, right?"

"Of course we'll be there," my mom said. "We're going out to dinner tonight, but that's much later. You know, we haven't seen your tap-dancing routine yet. Do you want to practice it for us now?"

"Oh, I'm not doing that anymore," I told my parents. "I've got something better. Something I'm more talented at."

My parents asked me what it was, but I told them it was a surprise. "You're going to love it, though!" I promised them.

Then I brought Bean Sprout into my room to practice.

"Once upon a time, there was a guy named Elvis," I started. "His job was to sing and dance around until girls fell on the floor grabbing their hearts and wishing to marry him."

Then I pretended to play a guitar and sang the first line of the "hound dog" song and that was it. Squash went all historical, laughing so hard I thought he might spit up his Cheerios.

We first found out how funny my brother thinks this is about a year ago. I had seen the Elvis guy on an old TV show with my parents one night. The next day, I did the act for Spinach and he cracked up. I didn't know what the second line of the song was, but it didn't matter because whatever I sang next—"Cracking at the top," "Yogurt in your shoes"—made him laugh even harder.

Now my parents call my Elvis act "The Old Standby." Whenever my brother is in a bad mood, they call me in to perform.

Because it only works if I do it. If my parents try, he just stares at them as if he's trying to remember who they are. Once, Margaret tried and he ran into his room and hid under his bed and I had to drag him out by his feet.

"Hound dog," I sang again. "Dooby, dooby, curtain!"

Carrot flopped onto my bed. He was laughing so hard tears squirted out of his eyes.

Then I got the leash. "Sorry. Margaret's teacher might make you wear it," I told him. "But don't worry, it's not for your neck." I buckled the leash around his overall straps in the back and waited to see what he thought.

He got up on his hands and knees. "Arf! I'm a dog!"

"No, you're not a dog," I told him.

"Grrrrrrr . . . I'm a dog!"

And then I saw what a wonderful idea that was! "Okay, fine. You're a dog. Just remember that tonight you're a dog who thinks Elvis is funny."

We practiced with the leash on for a while, and that went great. Then, while Potato had his nap, I

practiced saying, "My act is called 'Elvis and the Laughing Dog,'" and that went great, too.

Just before four o'clock, I reminded my dad that I needed a ride to rehearsal. "Oh, and Onion needs to come, too."

"First of all, your brother's name isn't Onion. And second of all, why does he need to come?"

So I had to tell my dad about my act. "But don't tell Mom yet, okay? It's going to be a great surprise for her!"

"No, I'm definitely not going to tell your mom. But we're also definitely not bringing your brother to that rehearsal. Because he's definitely not going to be up on that stage on a leash!"

"But he loves it! He thinks he's a dog!"

"Trust me on this. It's out of the question, Sport."

"But—"

"No buts. Now get in the car—it's almost four."

Then I made a big mistake: I got into the car. I was thinking so hard about how this was the unluckiest day of my life that I forgot to think about how much unluckier it could get if I went to the rehearsal.

When I walked into the auditorium, I saw Margaret's teacher and Mrs. Rice sitting at the side of the stage on tall director's chairs. I tried to hide, but Margaret's teacher saw me. She looked down at her clipboard and frowned. Then she yelled so loud all the kids in the auditorium stopped what they were doing to listen.

"Clementine, I don't seem to have you listed here. No matter, we'll fit you in. What's your act?"

I went over there and whispered in her ear that I didn't have one. I hoped the kids watching thought I was saying I couldn't choose one because I had too many talents.

"What do you mean, you don't have one?"
Margaret's teacher yelled, even though I was right
there.

Okay, fine. Maybe she didn't yell it. But all the
kids were listening so hard, they heard anyway.

"Hey, Clementine," one of the fourth graders
called out. "Your face
looks like it's burning
up! Maybe that could
be your act!"

About a million kids
laughed, even though
he was N-O-T, *not*
funny. But he was
right—when I get
embarrassed my face
gets red and hot. So I
didn't yell anything
back to him. I just

stood there with my red, hot face hanging down.

Mrs. Rice called me over. "Come sit beside me, Clementine," she said. "You can keep me company during the rehearsal."

So I had to sit in between Mrs. Rice and Margaret's teacher, right there at the side of the stage where all the kids could see me and know that I had no talents.

The first act was called A Dozen Doozie Cartwheelers. Twelve kids lined up, six on each side of the stage.

"Wait!" I yelled. I ran into the gym and dragged a tumbling mat back into the auditorium. I placed it on the floor in front of the stage. Then I got some of the Dozen Doozies to help me. Pretty soon we had all the mats piled up.

Margaret's teacher was glaring at me. She tapped her watch.

"They're going over," I explained. "No matter how they start off aiming, some of them are going over."

And they did. At least half a dozen of the Doozies went flying off the stage and right onto the mats. As soon as we got those kids back up and checked them for broken bones, I saw something else with my amazing corner-eyes.

"Stop!" I yelled. Then I ran over and grabbed a handful of Saltines from one of the third graders just before they went into his mouth.

"You're up next," I reminded him. "And you're whistling 'Yankee Doodle Dandy.' No crackers!"

When I got back, Margaret's teacher gave me a look that said she was going to remember all this nonsense when I got into her grade.

But Mrs. Rice gave me a thumbs-up. "Thank you, Clementine," she said. "Those crackers could have been a problem."

And you will not believe what happened next: Margaret's teacher apologized!

"I'm sorry," she said. "I'm a little antsy tonight."

I wanted to stick around to hear about why she was antsy, but just then I noticed that the Super-Duper Hula-Hoopers had been Hula-Hooping for a while. I went over and asked them how long they were planning to go on.

The girl on the right said, "I once went for five hours and thirteen minutes."

The girl on the left made a face that said, "That's nothing!"

"Well, you need to have an ending tonight," I said. "There are a lot of acts after yours." I borrowed the jump-ropers' CD player and explained about how they could Hula-Hoop to the music and then S-T-O-P, *stop* when it was over.

And I didn't even get to sit down again for the rest of the afternoon because everybody needed my help for something. Finally, after everyone had a chance to practice their acts, I went over to Mrs. Rice.

"May I go into your office and use the phone? I need to call my parents and tell them not to come."

"I think it's a little late for that." Mrs. Rice showed me her watch and then called out, "Take your places, people. Five minutes to showtime!"

Everybody ran to their places. I ran to the curtains and peeked out: every seat in the audience was filled.

Margaret's teacher clapped her hands for attention.

"Before we get started," she said, "I just want to thank you all for being part of the show. Each and every one of you is helping to raise money for the big school trip next spring. Except Clementine."

Okay, fine, she didn't actually say, "Except Clementine," but you could see everyone was thinking it.

Just then, the secretary came over and handed her a note.

"Oh! Oh, my goodness!" she cried. She jumped up out of her seat faster than I thought a grown-up should. "Oh, my goodness gracious, it's now! My daughter's having her baby! My first grandchild!"

"Go," said Mrs. Rice. "It's all right. We can handle the show. Just go be with your daughter."

"Oh, thank you!" Margaret's teacher said. And

then she left so fast she really did lose one of her bobby pins. It didn't look like lightning, though. It just looked like a bobby pin falling to the floor.

"Wow," I said to Mrs. Rice. "So now you have to run the whole show by yourself."

"No, not by myself," Mrs. Rice said. "I have an assistant. And that's you."

"Me? Oh, no. I can't!"

"You can. And I'm certainly not doing this alone."

"I really can't. I don't pay attention, remember?"

"You do pay attention, Clementine. Not always to the lesson in the classroom. But you notice more about what's going on than anyone I know. And that's exactly what I need tonight."

"I don't think this is a very good idea at all."

"Well, I do think it's a good idea. I'll prove it to you." Principal Rice called over one of the Hula-Hoopers. "Hillary, what's the second act after intermission?"

Hillary looked around. "I don't have a program," she said. "Do you want me to get you one?"

Mrs. Rice told her No thanks, then she turned to me. "Clementine, what's the second act after intermission?"

"Caleb from the fourth grade is going to burp 'The Star-Spangled Banner'," I told her.

"Does he need any props?"

"A two-liter bottle of root beer."

"How long will it take?"

"Forty-one seconds. Forty-eight if he has to stop to drink extra soda at the 'rockets' red glare' part."

"I rest my case," Principal Rice said. She pointed a "no buts" finger at the empty director's chair.

When a principal orders you to do something, it is impossible to refuse. Some part of you

always gives in. So I climbed into the chair.

"Open the curtains!" Principal Rice said. And the worried scribbling feeling exploded all through my body.

CHAPTER

9

Well, you would think those kids had never had a rehearsal.

First thing: all Dozen Doozies cartwheeled off the edge of the stage. Well, except for one girl, who forgot to move at all. Maria and Morris-Boris-Norris, from my class, went on next, and they cartwheeled right off the stage, too.

Nobody had to go to the emergency room, though, and the audience thought the whole thing was supposed to happen that way, so it was okay.

The next act was the O'Malley twins. Lilly had convinced Willy not to do the thing with his lunch, and to play a duet on the piano with her instead. But when Lilly got up to the mike to announce the act, she got so nervous she threw up.

I looked at Willy, sitting on the piano bench. Willy does everything Lilly does. And sure enough, he was getting ready.

"Not on the piano!" I yelled. Just in time.

Then I ran over and closed the curtains quick, so the whole audience wouldn't get started, too.

When the janitor came running out to clean everything up, I had a good idea.

"Send Sidney out now, in front of the curtains," I told Mrs. Rice.

"Why?" she asked. "There's no microphone out there."

"That's okay. Sidney's really loud. And she's going to recite a poem so there's no cartwheeling, just standing still. Besides, she's got really skinny feet, so she can fit out there if she stands sideways."

So Sidney went onstage and stood sideways and yelled her poem. By the time she was done, the stage was all mopped clean.

Next came the Hula-Hoopers, and they completely forgot what I'd told them about stopping. The music ended, but they just kept on going. Finally, I had to close the curtains to pull them off the stage so the jump-ropers could go on.

The jump-ropers must have figured that if the Hula-Hoopers didn't have to stop at the end of the music, neither did they. So I had to close the curtains on them, too.

Then came Margaret.

She did fine at the walking-on-stage-on-time thing, which not everybody did. But just as she got to the microphone, Alan took a picture of her from the audience. Which was a bad mistake.

Whenever anyone takes a picture of Margaret that she isn't expecting, she freezes. She says it's the horror of not knowing if she looks perfect or not. Which I don't understand, because Margaret always looks perfect.

No matter, there she was, frozen on the stage with her mouth hanging open. For one tiny second, a little part of me thought, *Good! No showing off for you tonight!*

But then my empathetic part took over.

I ran over to where Margaret could see me and waved until I got her eyes to unfreeze. I pointed to my hair and pretended to brush it.

Margaret nodded like a robot. She turned to the audience. "First, always brush your hair. Even if it's cut off like mine."

She looked back at me. I pretended to do up some buttons, then I pointed to my right.

"Always make sure you're buttoned up right," Margaret told the audience.

Then I lifted my foot and crossed my fingers over my sneaker.

"Never wear green sneakers!" Margaret said. "Green sneakers are the worst!" Then she shook herself, as if she'd been asleep. She went up closer to the mike.

"Wait a minute," she said. "I was just kidding about that one. You can wear any color sneakers you want. And green is the most fashionable of all."

She zoomed me a smile so huge all her teeth-bracelets sparkled like diamonds in the spotlight. I zoomed her one back—except with no teeth-bracelets because I don't have them yet. After that, Margaret was okay.

I went back and climbed up onto the director's chair, and Principal Rice gave me a huge smile, too. She leaned over and said, "I have the answer for you now, Clementine. About why you can't have a substitute. It's because there is no substitute for you. You are one of a kind!"

And that's when I realized I didn't have the worried feeling anymore. Instead, I had the proud feeling: like the sun was rising inside my chest.

The proud, sun-rising feeling stayed with me all through the rest of the show. And no matter what went wrong, which was plenty, Mrs. Rice and I just fixed it.

Finally we got to the last act, which was Joe and Buddy. Joe blew one note into his harmonica and Buddy started howling. The audience went wild for them, and kept calling for more, which was good because Buddy kept howling as if he'd been waiting for this all his life.

I felt a little jealous thinking about how great Spinach would have been up there with that fancy leash, and how much the audience would have loved my act, too. Especially my parents. Now that the last act was over, I guessed they were out there in the audience, going, "Hey! Wait a minute. Where was our daughter?"

Mrs. Rice and I closed the curtains and herded all the kids back onto the stage the way we had practiced. Then she opened the curtains again and

everybody took their bows, and only a few kids cracked their heads together.

Mrs. Rice and I stepped back into the wings and climbed up onto our chairs to watch.

The audience kept smiling and clapping, and the

kids kept smiling and bowing. And I was mostly happy, even though a little part of me was sad. Someday, I'd like to know what it feels like to have people clapping for me, too.

"We did it," I said to Principal Rice. "It's over, and we did it!"

"Yes, indeed, we did," said Principal Rice. "But it's not quite over. I have one more thing to do."

Then she got off her chair and went onstage to join the crowd of kids. I heard her take the microphone.

"Ladies and gentlemen, thank you for coming to Talent-Palooza, Night of the Stars. And now I would like to introduce the person who made it all possible . . . our very talented director. Without her, we would have had no show here tonight."

So Margaret's teacher had come back! It was

good news babies could be born so fast, in case I ever decided to have one, which I will not.

Mrs. Rice came over and put her hand on the side curtain. I jumped off the director's chair to make room for Margaret's teacher, even though I still didn't see her.

"Ladies and gentlemen," Mrs. Rice said, "please give a big round of applause for . . ."

She pulled open the curtain.

". . . *Clementine!*"

I was so surprised I just stood there staring. All the third and fourth graders were staring back at me . . . with thank-you eyes and big smiles.

Then they started clapping, regular at first, but then harder and harder. Pretty soon they were clapping so hard I was afraid some of the skinnier kids would break their wrists.

Then the audience started clapping like crazy,

too, and it seemed they were never going to stop. The sound grew so loud it practically peeled the ears right off my head. But I didn't care, because now I did know what it felt like to have people clapping for me: G-O-O-D, *good*.

On the way home, my mother kept shaking her head from being so astoundished. "I can't believe you kept that a secret all week, honey! You were so amazing!"

My dad caught my eye in the mirror and winked. "She's even more amazing than you know," he told my mother. "Yep, we have a very talented daughter here. Sport, we are so proud of you." Then he looked over at my mom and raised his eyebrows. She nodded and smiled.

"Are you tired, Clementine?" she asked. "Or do

you think you could stay up a little later than usual?"

"I'm not tired," I said. "Do you need me to spy on the sitter? Make sure she doesn't smoke cigars? Or order things from the Shopping Channel? Do you think she's making phone calls to Australia?" I might be a private detective when I grow up.

"No," said my dad. "The sitter's fine. We were wondering if you wanted to come to dinner with us at the Ritz, instead."

"Really?" I asked. "What about the peanuts?"

Usually, when my parents go out, it's my job to make sure the babysitter doesn't bring any peanuts and leave them around. Broccoli is allergic, and if he has even one tiny peanut, he might have to go to the hospital with his neck all blown up or something.

"We'll talk to the sitter," my dad said.

"I don't know," I said. My brother had never

been left with a sitter without me to save his life.

"It'll be all right, Clementine," my mother said. "We can trust the sitter to remember. We'd really like you to come. After all, we wouldn't even be going if it weren't for you."

So I said okay, and we went home and my parents got more dressed up. I didn't, because I already looked so great. My mom put on her new shoes, and I thought my dad was going to hurt his head from smacking it and saying, "Wow!"

When the babysitter came, my parents told her and told her about the peanuts. And then I told her and told her and told her, too. Then my dad looked at his watch and said, "We have reservations . . ." so we said good-bye.

But when we got to the lobby, I couldn't leave.

"Wait here." I hurried back to our apartment, got one of my mom's permanent markers, and

wrote on my brother's forehead, *NO PEANUTS
FOR ME!* in big, blue capital letters.

Then I felt all right.

On the way to the
restaurant, my parents
asked me what I wanted
for dinner. They always
do this so I don't have
to look at a menu and
have the not-choosing
problem.

"A hamburger and mashed potatoes," I said.

"I'm on it," said my dad.

And he was. My parents ordered food I had
never heard of. Then the waiter said, "And for the
young lady?" which was me. My dad ordered
some more food I had never heard of. But when it
came, it was a hamburger and mashed potatoes!

"Um, excuse me," I said, very politely. "May I also order some crackers?"

The waiter shook his head. "Sadly, there are no Ritz crackers at the Ritz. It is one of the deepest mysteries of the universe."

I didn't want him to feel embarrassed about that, so I told him I still liked his restaurant. "And I think you're a really good waiter, too. Very empathetic."

Which he was, because all night long, he figured out everything I was going to want and I never had to go up to the counter to ask for more anything, even ketchup.

For instance: exactly when we were all done with our meal and I was wondering about dessert, he magically appeared.

"I recommend three desserts tonight," he said. "The Boston cream pie, the crème brûlée, and the velvet chocolate cake are all especially good."

I could see my parents thinking, Oh, no, here comes the choosing thing.

But while the waiter was describing the desserts to us, his pencil drifted down to my menu and tapped one of the desserts for just an instant. I looked up and he winked.

"I'll have the velvet chocolate cake," I said.

My parents made I-don't-believe-it faces at each other. Then they ordered the other two desserts.

My dad's was crème brûlée, which is French for vanilla custard that's been blasted on the top with a blowtorch. I am not even kidding about that.

My mother's was the Boston cream pie, which came decorated with clementine slices.

"The clementine," said the waiter, "is the sweetest fruit, is it not?"

My mother laughed and nodded at me. "I've always thought so!"

She took one bite of her dessert and then said, "I just can't do it. I'm too full!"

My dad took one bite of his dessert and he said, "Me, too. I'm stuffed!"

Then they both pushed their plates over to me! So there I was at the Ritz-no-crackers restaurant, with three desserts!

"I think this is the luckiest day of my life," I told my parents.

Then my mother whispered, "Take off your sneakers."

So I did. And then secretly, under the table, she took off her purple dragonfly not-very-sensible wow shoes and slid them over to me. And for the rest of the meal I wore them, which nobody knew because I kept them under the tablecloth, even when the waiter came over to bring me more whipped cream.

Okay, fine. When the waiter came over to bring me more whipped cream, it is possible one of the dragonflies was peeking out.